STUCK IN THE MIDDLE

Check out these other L'il D books!

#1 It's All in the Name

#2 Take the Court

Coming soon:

#4 Out of Bounds

Hey L'il D!
STUCK IN THE MIDDLE

By Bob Lanier
and Heather Goodyear

Illustrated by
Desire Grover

A
LITTLE APPLE
PAPERBACK

SCHOLASTIC INC.
New York   Toronto   London   Auckland   Sydney
Mexico City   New Delhi   Hong Kong   Buenos Aires

I'd like to give a special shout-out to Mr. Lorrie Alexander, Director of the Masten Boys' Club, for his tireless patience, direction, discipline, and caring. His community outreach helped influence many of us in the neighborhood to make positive choices during critical stages in our development.
— B. L.

For Craig and Jeff — my terrific brothers, who've never excluded me.
— H. G.

No part of this publication may be reproduced in whole or in part, or stored in a retrieval system, or transmitted in any form or by any means, electronic, mechanical, photocopying, recording, or otherwise, without written permission of the publisher. For information regarding permission, write to Scholastic Inc., Attention: Permissions Department, 557 Broadway, New York, NY 10012.

ISBN 0-439-40901-2

Text copyright © 2003 by Bob Lanier
Illustrations copyright © 2003 by Scholastic Inc.
All rights reserved. Published by Scholastic Inc.
SCHOLASTIC, LITTLE APPLE, and
associated logos are trademarks and/or registered
trademarks of Scholastic Inc.

12 11 10 9 8 7   7 8/0

Printed in the U.S.A.
First printing, May 2003

Dear Reader,

Thank you for picking up this book. It's all about when I was a kid — back when people called me L'il Dobber, instead of Big Bob. Back before I played in the NBA.

I grew up in Buffalo, New York. I loved basketball and played every chance I got. Luckily, I had great friends to hang out with both on and off the court. We had a lot of fun adventures — and they're all included in these books.

Soon you'll meet me as a kid (remember, they call me L'il Dobber!). You'll also meet my friends Joe, Sam, and Gan. We are always up to something! We may not do the right thing all the time, but whatever we do, we learn from it. And we have a lot of fun!

And that's something I hope you do with this HEY L'IL D! book — have fun. Because believe me, reading is one of the most fun, most important things that you can do.

I hope you like my story.

Bob Lanier

Contents

Chapter 1
Running Late

Thwap, thwap, thwappita-thwap. The sound of a basketball echoed off the sidewalk as L'il Dobber walked along Northland Avenue on his way to school.

Sirens *blare*, lions *roar*, and L'il Dobber — who never seemed to be without a ball — went *thwap, thwap, thwap.*

He dribbled with his right hand, then shifted easily to his left. Between his legs, behind his back. Never breaking stride, never pausing to slow down. L'il Dobber dribbled a basketball the way most people breathe — without thinking, without effort. *Thwap, thwap, thwap.*

Maybe that's why he and his friend Gan Xu didn't hear Joe Crantz shouting until he caught up with them. "Whew," Joe wheezed, huffing and puffing. Joe bent down, hands on his knees, trying to catch his breath. "Didn't you hear me?" Joe asked. "I've been calling your names for two blocks."

L'il Dobber and Gan waited for their reddish-blond, freckle-faced friend to catch his breath. "I even yelled 'BOB LANIER,'" Joe said, "just to see if that might get your attention."

L'il Dobber smiled. "Hardly anyone calls me by my full name, except my parents when I'm in trouble," he said.

Joe nudged his friend's arm. "Trouble, huh? That happens sometimes."

L'il Dobber laughed. "Yeah, I guess it does. But getting *into* really big trouble isn't worth it, when getting *out* of trouble means my folks start using my full name. Nope, when my mom and Dit get unhappy, it's not much fun to be Bob Lanier."

"You call your Dad 'Dit,' right? How

come you don't call him Big Dobber, like everybody else?" asked Gan.

"Don't know," L'il Dobber answered with a shrug. "When he was a high school basketball star, everybody called him Big Dobber. That's why they call me L'il Dobber — because I'm going to be a b-ball star, too."

The three boys continued walking along Northland Avenue. The closer they got to school, the more crowded the sidewalk got. All the kids were out. The sun was warm and bright, which in Buffalo, New York, was something to celebrate. L'il Dobber's home-town was practically *famous* for having bad weather all the time. So when the sun shone, everybody seemed to be smiling.

"We waited at the corner for a while, then figured you weren't coming," Gan explained to Joe. "Why were you so late?"

"Don't get me started," Joe warned.

"Started about what?" Gan asked.

"My sister," Joe complained. "I spent the whole morning waiting for her to get out of the bathroom. She was in there staring in the mirror and combing her hair for, like, nine hours."

"That doesn't sound like Sam to me," L'il Dobber said. "Since when does your twin care what her hair looks like?"

"Since this morning." Joe sighed. "She must've changed her outfit five times!"

"Wow," said L'il Dobber. "That sounds like my sister, Geraldine."

"That sounds like every sister in the world," Gan said. "And I should know — I've got two of them. Believe me, Joe, you can say good-bye to that bathroom right now, because you're never going to see it again!"

L'il Dobber spun the basketball on his finger, grinning widely. "Gan's right, Joe. My parents and I have to beg Geraldine just to let us brush our teeth. She's in the bathroom all morning."

"But both your sisters are older," said Joe. "Sam's the same age as me. She can't tell me what to do."

"I bet she will!" said L'il Dobber. He and Gan laughed.

"Well, from now on, Sam will be leaving for school all by herself," Joe declared. "I'm not going to be late meeting you again — with all that running, I feel like I already had P.E.!"

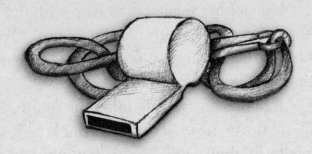

Chapter 2
The Big News

L'il Dobber and his friends had two favorite parts of school. One was recess. That's when they got to play ball. The other was P.E. class.

L'il Dobber got especially excited when he walked into P.E. today. His teacher, Mr. Johnson, stood tall in the middle of the gym with a basketball tucked under his arm. His white T-shirt said "St. Bonaventure Basketball." Mr. Johnson always matched his T-shirts to what they were learning in P.E., so L'il Dobber knew class was going to be great today.

"Line up in your squads." Mr. Johnson's booming voice echoed through the gymnasium.

L'il Dobber jogged to line up with the five other kids in squad number four. "We're starting our basketball unit today," Mr. Johnson told the class.

Whoops and cheers filled the room.

"For the next five weeks, you'll be learning basketball skills and having practice games," Mr. Johnson explained.

L'il Dobber smiled. He turned and caught Joe's and Gan's eyes, and they smiled back.

"At the end of the unit," said Mr. Johnson, while thumping the basketball in his hands, "we're going to demonstrate our new skills in a special afternoon game. Hopefully, many of your family members will be able to come and watch you play. Your class will play Mr. Martin's fourth grade class during the last hour of school."

Mr. Johnson walked back and forth in front of the squad lines. "Now listen up. Everybody will get a chance to play. I don't want to hear any complaints. You'll play together as teams and you'll support one another. Now for those of you who really love basketball" — he paused and looked at L'il Dobber — "I'll be holding tryouts right here after school on Friday to decide the starting lineup."

L'il Dobber glanced over at Joe and Gan.

They were smiling like it was the start of summer vacation.

Mr. Johnson gave a short, sharp toot on the whistle around his neck. "Pair up with someone in your squad," he ordered. "We'll practice the basics. I want one partner on the red line, the other partner opposite on the blue line. We'll start with the bounce pass."

L'il Dobber paired up with Jason Reich, a tall, skinny boy in his squad. Mr. Johnson tossed basketballs to everyone on the red line. He then marched across from a shy, curly-haired girl named Lizzie, and said, "This is the proper way to throw a bounce pass. Hold the ball with two hands at chest level, like this. Then step forward on one foot and bounce it — just one bounce — across to your partner."

Boom. He snapped a quick pass to Lizzie. L'il Dobber was surprised when Lizzie grabbed the ball and snapped it back to Mr. Johnson just as quickly.

"Understand?" Mr. Johnson asked. "I

don't want to see soft, lazy passes. Put some *oomph* behind it."

The sound of thumping basketballs filled the gym. It was like music to L'il Dobber's ears. All the while, Mr. Johnson strode up and down the two lines, barking comments — "Good, *that's* the way, L'il Dobber!" — or offering quiet advice to those who needed it.

Tweet! Mr. Johnson's whistle blew.

Everyone held their balls in silence. When Mr. Johnson blew his whistle, it was best to give him your full attention.

"Now, chest passes," Mr. Johnson ordered. Again, he snapped a hard pass through the air to Lizzie. This time, it bounced off her hands.

"Everyone give it a try," Mr. Johnson said, and the kids practiced their chest passes.

"No, no, no," Mr. Johnson yelled over the noise, shaking his head. "You've got to put some zip on that ball. Throw it like you mean it."

Tweet! It was time to practice dribbling.

Mr. Johnson set out cones across the gym floor. Everybody had to form two lines, then dribble across the entire gym, weaving through the cones as they went.

"This is cool!" whispered L'il Dobber as he took his place in line behind Joe.

"Yeah," Joe agreed. "We get to play ball and it's not even recess!"

L'il Dobber expertly dribbled the ball the length of the gym. He jogged and weaved, shifting the ball between his hands with ease.

When his turn was over, L'il Dobber carefully watched the other kids. Some were pretty good, but others . . . *yowch.* A lot bounced the basketball off their feet by accident, then had to chase the ball as it bounded across the floor. Poor Jeremy Patuto and Rachel Jordan, who weren't exactly future stars of the NBA, got tangled up with each other and fell to the floor.

Tweet!

"That's it for today," Mr. Johnson announced.

L'il Dobber looked across the gym and saw his teacher, Ms. Wilson, waiting at the door.

"Put the balls back in the rack and line up with your teacher," Mr. Johnson's big voice boomed. "Remember, everyone is welcome to come to tryouts this Friday after school. I'll be picking the starters for both teams — so bring your best game."

Chapter 3
Sam and Sarah

Lunch recess — for L'il Dobber, Gan, Joe, and Sam — meant one thing: a chance to play basketball on the school yard's court. The boys had just finished scraping their feet across the court to clear off the leaves that had fallen, when Sam walked up with another girl at her side.

"Hey, guys," Sam said. "Sarah's going to play with us today."

"Really?" asked L'il Dobber.

That was a surprise. Usually no one else played on the court with them. The boys eyed Sarah curiously and shrugged. Sure.

"Sarah wants to practice for the basketball unit in gym class," explained Sam. "She wants to be ready for the big game."

Sam and Sarah were both in Mr. Martin's class. They'd be playing against L'il Dobber's team at the end of the unit.

"Let's play, then," said L'il Dobber. He picked up his basketball from under the basket and snapped a chest pass to Sarah. She shrieked in alarm and jumped to the side.

Sam lunged and caught the ball before it bounced away.

"What are you doing?" asked L'il Dobber in surprise.

"The ball scared me," said Sarah, pushing her black, curly hair from her face.

L'il Dobber, Joe, and Gan started cracking up.

"Scared you, huh?" Joe asked, laughing.

"Yeah," Sarah admitted, a little embarrassed.

The boys kept laughing.

"Come on, guys," Sam said. "Stop laughing."

"But it's funny," said L'il Dobber.

"Then how come I'm not laughing?" challenged Sam. She threw the ball hard at L'il Dobber's chest.

"All right. Take it easy, Sam," L'il Dobber said.

"Let's start again," Joe said. "What do you know about basketball?" he asked Sarah.

"Not much," she answered. "I was hoping that maybe you guys could teach me." She paused. "My brother plays on the middle school team."

"Then why do you need us?" Gan asked politely. "He could coach you."

"He never lets me play," said Sarah. "He says girls aren't any good at playing ball."

The boys didn't have much to say to that. Finally Gan suggested, "How about if we just shoot around?"

"Yeah," L'il Dobber agreed. "But this time, I'll just hand you the ball — if you don't think that will be too scary," he said with a laugh.

"It won't bite," joked Joe.

Sarah held the ball very gently, like it was made of glass. Then she took a funny hop-step and sort of flung the ball skyward. It bounced five feet in front of the basket.

L'il Dobber, Joe, and Gan couldn't help themselves. They laughed again. Even Sam chuckled a little bit.

"Not very good, huh?" Sarah admitted.

"It's not exactly NBA style," L'il Dobber joked. When Sam shot him a look, he said, "But, um, it's a good start."

Everyone shot around for a while longer — though Sarah didn't even hit the hoop's rim once.

When the recess whistle sounded, the group headed back into school through the metal doors.

"Can I play again tomorrow?" Sarah asked.

"Sure, you can," Sam said right away. "Right, guys?"

Gan and Joe kept their eyes to the ground and their mouths shut. L'il Dobber hesitated, then said, "Um . . . yeah, sure, I guess."

"Great!" Sarah answered. She smiled happily as she and Sam turned into their classroom.

"Yeah, great," mumbled Joe. "Just great."

Chapter 4
Girls Can't Play

After dinner that night, the Laniers sat together eating homemade peach cobbler with vanilla ice cream. It was delicious.

"Sam brought a girl to play ball with us at lunchtime today," L'il Dobber said. He scraped the bottom of the bowl with his spoon.

"Is she as good as the rest of you?" asked his mom.

L'il Dobber shook his head. "No, she plays like a girl."

"Girls can play basketball," his big sister, Geraldine, protested.

"That's right," his mother agreed. "Sam's a good player, you've told me so yourself."

L'il Dobber shrugged. "Sam's different."

"Different?" his father asked.

"Sam doesn't play like a girl," L'il Dobber struggled to explain. "She's — I don't know — more like us."

His mother laughed softly. "I don't know about that," she said. "One of these days you boys are going to open your eyes and see that Sam is a beautiful young lady."

"Oh, Mom!" protested L'il Dobber. "It's not that. It's just — well, this girl, Sarah, she's not like Sam at all. She wears little thingies in her hair . . ."

"Clips," Geraldine corrected.

". . . and skirts and, you know, girl stuff," L'il Dobber noted. "She can't even dribble three times without messing up. And now she's going to waste all our time at recess."

His father cleared his throat. It was a signal that he wasn't happy with what L'il Dobber was saying.

"I want to work on my game, Dit," L'il
Dobber said to his dad. "How am I supposed
to get better, playing with a girl who doesn't
know a double dribble from a hook shot?"

"By teaching her, that's how," his dad
said.

"It won't be easy," said L'il Dobber.

"What does she know already?" asked
Mrs. Lanier.

"She knows what a basketball is, and that's about it," answered L'il Dobber.

"Come on," said Geraldine. "That's ridiculous."

"I'm serious!" protested L'il Dobber. "She can't catch, dribble, or shoot."

"Well, I give her credit for trying to learn — and so should you," his dad told him sternly.

"I give her credit for spending two minutes with you and your friends," Geraldine said to her brother.

"That's not nice, Geri," said Mrs. Lanier.

"Sorry, Mom," Geraldine replied. "But those boys think they invented basketball."

"What about you, Jerdine?" challenged L'il Dobber. "You're no good at ball, either."

"Am, too," Geraldine snapped back.

"Then how come you never play with Dit and me, huh?" asked L'il Dobber.

"Because you never ask me," Geraldine said. Then she rose from her seat to clear the dishes from the table.

"Oh," said L'il Dobber thoughtfully.

Sarah had said almost the same thing about her brother.

"Look, L'il Dobber," his dad said. "Teaching someone how to play can help make you better. It forces you to get back to basics."

L'il Dobber nodded, knowing he shouldn't disagree with Dit. But in his heart, he sure didn't see how helping Sarah was going to get him into the NBA.

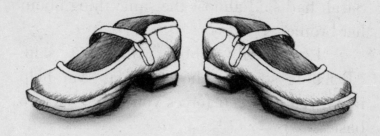

Chapter 5
High Heels and Basketball

L'il Dobber felt the basketball under his arm get pushed from behind.

"Heads up, L'il D!" Joe laughed as he joined his friends on their way to school the next morning.

"You're late again," Gan told Joe. "We almost left without you."

"Guess why I'm late," said Joe.

"Sam?" L'il Dobber and Gan asked together.

"You got it," said Joe. "I don't know what's going on with her these days. I had to leave her behind. She can hardly walk in her new shoes."

"What do you mean?" asked L'il Dobber. "Sam only wears sneakers."

"Not anymore," Joe answered. "I had to spend all last night at the mall waiting for her to pick out fancy new school clothes."

Gan rubbed his eyes and pretended to yawn really big. "You went to the mall with your sister? *Bor-ing!*"

"You said it," Joe agreed. "Sam's been begging my mom for new clothes for weeks now. So last night they dragged me around to a bunch of girls' stores."

"Ugh," said L'il Dobber. "That's the worst."

Joe shook his head. "The worst part was that Sam got three new outfits and two pairs of shoes . . . and I got nothing."

The minute L'il Dobber saw Sam and Sarah at lunch recess, he knew it was true.

"Hey, guys," the girls said. It sure didn't look like Sam. She had her hair down and hanging all around her shoulders, and she was wearing a fuzzy sweater and long skirt.

"What are you staring at?" asked Sam, with her hand on her hip.

A stranger, thought L'il Dobber.

But out loud he muttered, "Nothing."

"Well, what about you?" Sam asked, turning to Gan. "Do you have something to say?"

"You've gotten taller," Gan replied.

"It's those crazy shoes I told you about," Joe said. "Those clunky heels make her two inches taller."

"Let's just play ball," said L'il Dobber. "What do you want to learn today, Sarah?"

"Maybe I'll just watch for a couple days," Sarah answered. "Sam said you guys like to play two-on-two."

"Sounds good to me!" said L'il Dobber. He was excited that they would actually get to play a real game. "Let's make it Sam and Joe against me and Gan."

L'il Dobber threw the ball to Sam, who took it to the top of the court. Sam dribbled once, twice, gave a head fake and drove to her left. *Whoops, slam!* Sam twisted her ankle and fell to the ground.

L'il Dobber grabbed the ball. "Are you all right?" he asked.

Sam stood up immediately. She brushed

her skirt and smoothed her hair. "Yeah, I'm fine."

"I don't think playing ball in those shoes is such a good idea," L'il Dobber said.

"I said I'm fine," Sam repeated sharply.

"OK," said L'il Dobber doubtfully. He threw a nice bounce pass to Gan, who dribbled down and shot an easy layup.

Sam took the ball to the top of the key. Again, she tried to dribble left and lost one of her shoes. Frustrated, Sam threw a pass to Joe and put her shoe back on. Joe bounced the ball back to Sam, who glided past Gan for an easy shot.

"Guard her, Gan," said L'il Dobber.

The next time Sam had the ball, Gan just halfheartedly stuck out his arm to try and stop her.

"What are you doing?" asked L'il Dobber. "That's not how you play defense, Gan."

"I didn't want to grab her sweater," complained Gan.

"Why aren't you trying?" Sam asked Gan angrily. "You're *letting* me score."

"You're dressed like my sisters," Gan told her.

"So?" asked Sam.

"They'd throw a fit if I messed up their nice clothes," Gan said.

"Sam doesn't care," Joe spoke up. "Just play ball."

Gan looked at Sam.

"Just play ball," Sam agreed.

"Sorry," Gan apologized. "You just look so different today, playing in fancy clothes."

Sam glared at him. "Is that a problem?"

"It's a problem for *you*," L'il Dobber said, swiping the ball from Sam and spinning to shoot a turnaround jumper. *Swish.* "Because nobody in high heels beats L'il Dobber!"

Chapter 6
Tryouts

Tweet! Mr. Johnson's shrill whistle blared through the gym on Friday afternoon.

"Listen up," he barked. "If you're in Ms. Wilson's class, start warming up at the basket behind me. Mr. Martin's class, over there." He pointed to the far basket.

Excited about the tryouts, L'il Dobber, Joe, and Gan shot around with their group. Sam was in Mr. Martin's class, so she went to the far basket. L'il Dobber counted eleven kids from his class and eight kids from Sam's class at the other end.

After five minutes, Mr. Johnson called them all to center court. He set up different drills for each group. "I'll be watching and taking notes," he said in his no-nonsense style. "Just relax and try to do your best."

L'il Dobber, Gan, and Joe played great all afternoon. They hit almost all of their layups, dribbled well, and made a bunch of foul shots. "We'll make the starting five for sure," Joe whispered to L'il Dobber.

When he had a chance, L'il Dobber checked out the players from Mr. Martin's class. Something didn't look right. He watched Sam dribble slowly toward the basket, then throw an air ball.

"She shoots better than that," L'il Dobber said. "What's going on with her?" he asked Joe.

Joe shrugged, but then he watched his twin sister carefully. Sam hit three nice shots in a row. "Just nervous, I guess," Joe said.

But something definitely wasn't right. Sam kept missing easy shots — shots she normally could hit with her eyes closed.

For the rest of the tryouts, when it wasn't L'il Dobber's turn to be playing, he watched Sam. He saw her miss some easy jump shots,

but then make much harder ones. He was surprised when she sank five foul shots in a row, but then threw air balls on the next two.

She's not trying her best, thought L'il Dobber. *I don't understand it.*

After tryouts, L'il Dobber, Joe, and Gan waited outside in the hall. As soon as Sam appeared, they started in on her.

"Why'd you play so bad?" Gan asked.

"You didn't even try," Joe said.

"You might not even make the starting five," L'il Dobber said. "And you're one of the best players in your class."

"I know," Sam said quietly.

"You know?" Joe repeated.

"Yeah, and I don't care," mumbled Sam.

"What?!" L'il Dobber exclaimed.

"Maybe I don't want to be a starter," said Sam. "Sarah isn't a starter. And lots of other girls in my class tease me about playing so much basketball. They say it's for boys."

"Who cares what they say?" Joe responded. "You love playing ball, Sam."

"I *do* love basketball," Sam answered quietly. "But I like having friends, too."

"We're your friends," L'il Dobber pointed out.

"I mean *girl*friends," Sam said.

"That's crazy, Sam," Gan said. "Why do you —"

"Just stop bugging me, OK?" Sam interrupted. "All of you, just stop it," she snapped, her eyes flashing angrily.

"We will," Joe snapped back, "when you start being yourself again."

"I am *trying* to be myself!" shouted Sam. She shook her head, turned on her heel, and walked away.

B'Ball
Starting Players

1. Rasheed 1. Samantha
2. Jimmy   2. Thomas
3. Bob   3. Kevin
4. Gan   4. Brett
5. Joe . 5. William

Chapter 7
Stuck in the Middle

"As you leave gym class today, check the list on the wall," Mr. Johnson told L'il Dobber's class on Monday. "It names the starting five for each class."

"Squad one, line up," he instructed. "Two, three, four, and five follow them in order."

L'il Dobber could hardly stand still until squad four started moving.

Hurry up, hurry up, he silently urged the kids in front of him.

L'il Dobber made his way to the list and looked at the names for Ms. Wilson's class. He, Joe, and Gan were three out of the five.

"We all made it!" shouted L'il Dobber.

They whooped and jumped around with their hands in the air.

"Boys," said Ms. Wilson.

"Boys," called Ms. Wilson more loudly.

L'il Dobber, Joe, and Gan stopped jumping up and down. They turned to see the rest of the class lined up and waiting.

"Sorry, Ms. Wilson," said L'il Dobber as they quickly stepped into the back of the line.

"I understand," said Ms. Wilson and smiled. "I'm happy for you, too."

"Did you see that Sam made it?" whispered Joe as they walked through the hall.

"Good," L'il Dobber whispered back.

Later that day, Ms. Wilson sent L'il Dobber on an errand. He had to get some books from the main office. As he walked quietly along, he saw a group of girls come out of the bathroom up ahead. Sam and Sarah were two of them. They didn't notice L'il Dobber, and he was about to say hi until he heard what they were talking about.

"Why won't you come over to my house after school?" Brittany Benson, a small brown-haired girl in Mr. Martin's class, was asking Sam. "We're going to make friendship bracelets."

"I'd love to come, but . . . well, I've got basketball practice," Sam answered hesitantly. "The big game is coming up."

"I told you not to go to those starting

lineup tryouts," said Mindy Wasserman, another one of Sam's classmates. She flipped her long red hair back over her shoulder.

"Now we'll never get to see you," Brittany chimed in. "You'll be the only girl out there with all of those boys."

Sarah disagreed. "I think it's *great* that you made it, Sam."

"Great?" Mindy asked. "Now she'll be practicing even more. Sam will *never* have time to hang out with the girls."

"Mindy is right," echoed Brittany, elbowing Sam gently in the arm. "You'll miss all the fun. Or don't you like being one of the girls, Sam?"

"Oh, I do," Sam said. "I love hanging out with you. It's just that . . ."

"It's just . . . *what?*" asked Mindy.

"It's just that I love basketball, too," Sam explained.

"You should watch her play sometime," Sarah told the girls. "Sam is really talented."

The girls turned right down the hallway. L'il Dobber watched them go, thinking about what he'd heard. Thanks to those girls, Sam was stuck in the middle between her girlfriends and basketball.

He wondered which she would choose.

Chapter 8
A Talk with Geraldine

That night, L'il Dobber went into the living room after dinner. He found Geraldine lying on the sofa with her nose in a book. L'il Dobber flopped down into the chair next to her.

"I need to ask you something," he said.

"What?" Geraldine asked absently, without looking up from her book.

"Do you ever get picked on for being a track star at school?"

"No. Why would I?" asked Geraldine. She turned a page in her book.

"Because sports are for boys," said L'il Dobber.

That got Geraldine's attention. She put

down the book. "How do you figure that?" she asked.

"That's what a lot of guys at school say."

"Well, boys *would* say that," Geraldine sneered.

"It's not just the boys," L'il Dobber replied. "Some girls say it, too."

"Those are just the girls who don't like sports," said Geraldine. "I don't pay any attention to talk like that. But what's up, L'il D? Why are you asking me all this stuff?"

L'il Dobber felt glad to have someone to talk to about this — even if it was his sister. "Sam used to play only with Joe, Gan, and me," he explained. "But lately, she's been hanging out with lots of girls. She wears new clothes and Joe says she's doing her hair *every* morning."

"What's wrong with that?" Geraldine asked. "It wouldn't hurt you guys to dress a little nicer and use a comb once in a while."

"That's not what I'm talking about," said L'il Dobber.

Geraldine sighed. "Then what are you talking about?"

"All I'm trying to say is that Sam wants the girls in her class to like her. But I heard how they talk to her, and, well, I can't figure out why she would *want* them as friends. They want her to change and be more like them. And, um, we like her just the way she is."

Geraldine sat up straight and looked her brother in the eye. "Sam still plays ball with you, right?" she said.

"Yeah," L'il Dobber admitted.

"And she's still a good basketball player and friend, no matter what she looks like or what girls she talks to, right?" Geraldine said.

"Yeah," L'il Dobber confessed.

"So there's no problem," Geraldine concluded. "Just be her friend by letting her be herself. After all, you know, Sam might not want to spend her whole *life* on the basketball court — not like some people I know."

Geraldine gave L'il Dobber a friendly punch on the shoulder. She picked up her

book again and snuggled deeper into the couch cushions.

"Hey, Jerdine," said L'il Dobber.

"I'm trying to read here," Geraldine answered.

L'il Dobber paused. "Um, maybe next time Dit and I play basketball, you could play with us, too."

Geraldine looked up at him. "That might be fun," she said.

L'il Dobber smiled. He couldn't believe he'd just had a helpful conversation with Geraldine. It was an all-time first. Maybe, just maybe, having a big sister could be all right sometimes.

Chapter 9
Playing a Little "D"

"Hey, guys," Sam said quietly as she walked up to the basketball court at recess the next day.

"Where's Sarah?" asked Gan.

"I wasn't sure you guys wanted us to play," said Sam.

"Why not?" asked L'il Dobber.

"You seemed mad about the tryouts, and that I wasn't as excited as you guys about making the starting five," she said.

"It didn't look like you tried your best," observed Gan.

Sam shrugged. "Well, yeah, I was a little confused, I guess. But I've been talking about it with my mom and with Sarah, and now I'm happy I made it. I still love basketball," Sam said. "I just want to do girl stuff sometimes, too."

"Maybe we were a little confused, too," said L'il Dobber. "We thought you were changing too much."

Gan added, "You're still our friend — no matter what you wear."

"And you're still a good ballplayer," said Joe. "And a great sister," he mumbled shyly.

Sam smiled — a big, wide, happy smile.

"Now go get Sarah, and let's play some ball," said L'il Dobber.

"I'll be right back," Sam said. "And you better be ready, 'cause I'm back in tennis shoes today!" She sprinted across the school yard to find Sarah.

For the next two weeks, Sam and Sarah practiced hard with the boys. Sam was on fire — spinning to the hoop, making tough shots — she was playing great ball. Even Sarah was slowly getting better. And the boys found that they liked teaching her about the game. It did force them to think about the basics of basketball, just as L'il Dobber's dad had said. And now Sarah could catch a pass, dribble pretty well, and even make a layup once in a while.

But her shooting from outside was still . . . well, awful.

"I'll never be good enough for the game next week," Sarah said, after tossing up another air ball from the foul line. "I'll never make any baskets."

L'il Dobber grabbed the ball and held it in his hands. "Some people think you're only good at basketball if you score a lot of points," he said to Sarah. "But that's not true."

"It's not?" asked Sarah.

"It's just as important to play strong 'D,'" he said.

"Strong . . . what?" asked Sarah.

"Strong 'D' — as in defense. If you're good at defense, you can really help your team a lot," explained L'il Dobber.

Sarah nodded. "So how do I learn defense?"

"The big thing is, when the other team has the ball, you've got to keep them from scoring by staying between the ball and the basket. To do that, you have to be able to move side to side quickly," Joe told Sarah.

Joe demonstrated by getting into the defensive position. "Put your legs wide, like this, bend your knees, and kind of crouch down," he instructed.

Sarah tried it and caught on immediately.

"You got it!" exclaimed Sam. "Now shuffle your feet to one side, then the other. Keep your arms up."

"It's a little like dance class," Sarah said. "I can do this easily. It's the ball that gives me problems."

"Now stand in front of me," said L'il Dobber. He began to dribble slowly at the top of the court. Sarah stepped up to guard him. "That's good," L'il Dobber praised. "Now I'm going to try and dribble past you. But you

shuffle and stay in front of me. Remember, try to stay between me and the basket."

L'il Dobber dribbled slowly, and Sarah shuffled in front of him as he moved toward the basket. L'il Dobber then tried dribbling faster and faster. But each time he turned, Sarah blocked his path to the hoop.

"Awesome 'D,' Sarah!" Sam shouted.

"Thanks, guys. You're the best," Sarah said. Her eyes gleamed with pride. "Maybe I can play a little 'D' after all!"

Sarah smiled as the whistle blew, signaling the end of recess. "Hey, Sam, I've . . . er . . . got something for you." Sarah reached into her pocket. "It's a friendship bracelet," she explained. "I made it for you last night."

Sam squealed with delight and turned to show it to the boys. They just nodded. "It's beautiful!" she gushed. "Thanks, Sarah. You're a great friend."

"So are you, Sam," Sarah said. "And you're a pretty great ballplayer, too."

Chapter 10
The Big Game

L'il Dobber and Gan peeked through the hallway door into the crowded gymnasium. Today was the day of the big game.

"Look at all of the people!" said Gan excitedly.

"Playing in front of a big crowd will be a blast," said L'il Dobber. He pointed to the bleachers. "Look, there's my mom and dad, sitting next to your parents."

"There's Sam and Joe's mom," Gan noticed. "I'm glad they all took off from work to watch us play."

Tweet, tweet! Mr. Johnson whistled two sharp blasts and the teams ran into the gym.

"Welcome to our fourth grade basketball matchup," Mr. Johnson told the crowd. "The classes have been working hard, and we're proud to give you a friendly demonstration of how well we play the game."

The crowd stomped their feet on the bleachers and cheered.

Mr. Johnson introduced the teams, naming each player to a fresh round of applause. Then he introduced the starters.

"For Ms. Wilson's class," Mr. Johnson yelled in his booming voice, "Rasheed Shealing, Gan Xu, Joseph Crantz, Jimmy Lewis, and Bob Lanier!" L'il Dobber ran to join his team at center court when his name was called.

"For Mr. Martin's class, Samantha Crantz, Thomas Banks, Brett Williams, Kevin Lewis, and William Brown!"

The two teams shook hands and went to their benches for the national anthem. Then the game began.

Mr. Johnson threw the jump ball up to start the game and L'il Dobber easily tipped it to Joe. Joe dribbled down the court and scored the first basket of the game for their team.

It was a close game all the way. L'il Dobber blocked shots, got rebounds, and made a lot of baskets. In fact, everyone seemed to be playing their best. And the crowd enjoyed every minute of it, clapping and cheering all the big plays.

Sam took the ball, faked a drive, pulled up, and sank a ten-foot jump shot. "You're playing great today," L'il Dobber whispered to Sam as they jogged to the other end of the court.

"Thanks," said Sam. "So are you."

By halftime, L'il Dobber's team was ahead by eight points. The starting ten players had stayed in for most of the first half, until Mr. Johnson began putting in substitutes to make sure every player in the class got time on the floor. When it was L'il Dobber's turn to sit out, he watched the game closely.

With two minutes left in the game, it was still close. Sam and Thomas Banks had led their team back by making a series of tough shots when they had fallen behind. They were losing by only three points.

L'il Dobber and Gan sat nervously on the sideline, watching Joe dribble down the floor.

As Joe started toward the basket, Sarah stepped out to guard him. Joe tried to dribble left, but Sarah shuffled in front of him. Joe tried to dribble right, but Sarah blocked his way.

Joe paused, frustrated by Sarah's tough defense, when suddenly Sarah reached out and poked the ball from his hands. She passed it to Thomas, who raced down the court to score a basket.

Even though Sarah was on the other team, L'il Dobber couldn't help but be proud of her play. "We taught her to play 'D' like that," he whispered to Gan on the bench.

"Way to go, Sarah!" Gan yelled.

With ten seconds left in the game, L'il Dobber's team was ahead by just one point. Sam dribbled slowly as the seconds ticked down, searching for a way to the hoop. There was no one open for her to pass to.

The crowd began to count down the seconds. "Six . . . five . . . four . . . three . . ."

Sam suddenly faked right, causing her defender to lose his balance. Then she picked up the ball, jumped, and shot the ball up into the air.

Swish!

The gymnasium erupted with cheers and shouts. The whistle sounded — game over. All of Sam's teammates ran onto the floor, jumping wildly and hugging Sam.

L'il Dobber, Joe, and Gan sat disappointed with the rest of their team. But as they watched the celebration, each boy felt a mix of emotions. It was a drag to lose. But they felt good for Sam. She sure looked happy.

L'il Dobber's parents came down from the bleachers to greet them. "Hi, Mom. Hi, Dit," L'il Dobber said quietly.

"You played terrific!" L'il Dobber's mom cheered and squeezed him on the shoulders.

"We lost, though," groaned L'il Dobber.

Dit grinned. "You *all* played well. It was just Sam's day, no big deal," he said. "You all have a lot to be proud of."

Sam, wearing a big smile on her face, walked up with her mom.

"Awesome shot!" Joe told her. He gave his twin sister a hug.

"Amazing," Gan said.

"Thanks, guys," said Sam.

As they all walked out of the gym together, two voices called out to Sam from the bleachers.

"Wait, Sam!" yelled Mindy and Brittany.

The group stopped walking as Sam turned to face her friends in surprise.

Mindy hugged Sam. "We wanted to tell you what an awesome job you did." She bit her bottom lip as she smiled up at Sam. "Now we see why you spend so much time playing basketball," she said apologetically.

"Yeah," said Brittany. "You sure played great for a girl today."

"Are you kidding?" replied L'il Dobber. He put his arm around Sam's shoulders and squeezed. "Sam plays great for anybody!"

Tell us about your next adventure!

OUT OF BOUNDS

Monday after school, L'il Dobber was throwing his basketball against the side of his house and seeing how high it would bounce back to him. He had just pumped it full of air, and if he hit the base of the house just right the ball bounced so high he had to jump to catch it.

Shwip, shwip, shwip.

The sound of Mr. Palmer's hedge clippers floated over the fence from next door. L'il

Dobber pictured him hacking away any branches that dared to stick out of his perfectly designed bushes.

L'il Dobber threw the ball hard at the base of his house.

"Hi, L'il D!" came a yell from the street. L'il Dobber turned to see Gan waving out the van window as he drove past with his family.

L'il Dobber waved back and the ball bounced over his head. It sailed through the air and disappeared into Mr. Palmer's front yard.

L'il Dobber sighed. "Uh, oh."

He crept across his driveway to the side of Mr. Palmer's house and peeked around the corner at the front yard. No basketball.

L'il Dobber dared to stick his head out a little farther and then he saw his ball. Sitting right in the middle of the flowers it had crushed when it rolled over them.

The hedge clippers suddenly stopped.

"Uh, oh." L'il Dobber sighed again. Mr. Palmer had seen the ball, too.

L'il Dobber whipped his head back

around the corner and flattened himself against the side wall of the house. He didn't know what to do.

Slowly, he tiptoed back across the driveway. He silently opened the back door and crept through. Then, just as silently, he closed the door behind him.

"Mom," L'il Dobber whispered.

His mom stood at the kitchen counter making chicken for dinner. She turned and gave him a puzzled look. "What?" she whispered back.

"My ball went into Mr. Palmer's yard," L'il Dobber said.

"Why are you whispering?" asked his mom, still whispering herself.

"So he won't hear me."

Mrs. Lanier smiled and said in a normal voice, "You're inside now. I don't think he can."

"Oh, yeah." L'il Dobber smiled, too. "So what should I do?"

"Go ask for your ball back."

"From the Grouch?" L'il Dobber asked in disbelief.

"Bobby . . ." L'il Dobber's mom scolded and shook a raw chicken leg at him.

"It also smashed some flowers," L'il Dobber admitted.

"Then you'd better apologize, too," said his mother. She went back to cleaning the chicken in the sink.

L'il Dobber could see his mom wasn't going to give him an idea that he would like any better, so he turned and trudged back out the door. He kept trudging all the way to his neighbor's front yard.

Mr. Palmer's bright green-and-yellow flannel shirt looked a lot happier than his face when he turned from picking up smashed flowers and saw L'il Dobber standing by the fence.

"I'm not giving your ball back," he told L'il Dobber right away.

L'il Dobber was so surprised that he forgot to be nervous and blurted out, "Why?!"

"Do you see what you did to my flowers?" Mr. Palmer growled and held up a bunch of flowers with broken stems.

"Yes," L'il Dobber said quietly. "And I came to apologize."

Mr. Palmer stared at him with his gray eyes. They made L'il Dobber very uneasy and suddenly, he was tongue tied.

"Well, are you going to apologize?" Mr. Palmer asked.

"Yes, yes, I am," L'il Dobber stammered. "I'm sorry."

"I accept your apology," Mr. Palmer said gruffly. "I need to put these in some water." He took the crumpled flowers and walked up his porch steps.

Mr. Palmer had already pulled open the screen door before L'il Dobber could ask, "Can I have my ball back now?"

"So you can ruin more of my flowers? I don't think so."

About the Authors

Bob Lanier is a basketball legend and a member of the Basketball Hall of Fame. A graduate of St. Bonaventure University, he has been hailed as much for his work in the community as for his play on the court. Winner of numerous awards and honors, he currently serves as Special Assistant to NBA Commissioner David Stern and as Captain of the NBA's All-Star Reading Team.

Like L'il Dobber, Bob has faced life's challenges head-on with a positive attitude and a never-ending belief in the power and value of reading and education.

Bob and his wife, Rose, have eight children and reside in Scottsdale, Arizona.

Heather Goodyear started creative writing in the first grade, with poems she wrote on scraps of paper. Her teacher gave her a blank notebook and said, "Be sure to let me know when you publish your first book." Hey L'il D! is her first series.

Sports were an important part of Heather's childhood in Michigan. As the only girl in a close family with two brothers, she learned early to hold her own in living room wrestling matches, driveway basketball contests, and family football games.

Heather says that this love of sports and her classroom experience as a teacher make Hey L'il D! especially fun for her to write.

Heather lives in Arizona with her husband, Chris, and their three young children.